Uncle
Fred Is a
Knucklehead!

Dan Gutman

Pictures by
Jim Paillot

HARPER

An Imprint of HarperCollinsPublishers

To Emma

Thanks to Jamie Greifenberger, Heidi Margaret, Kathy Yannul Crump, Ray, Craig, and Howard.

My Weirdtastic School #2: Uncle Fred Is a Knucklehead!
Text copyright © 2023 by Dan Gutman
Illustrations copyright © 2023 by Jim Paillot

Library of Congress Control Number: 2022944218
ISBN 978-0-06-320696-0 (pbk bdg) — ISBN 978-0-06-320697-7 (trade bdg)

Typography by Laura Mock
23 24 25 26 27 PC/CWR 10 9 8 7 6 5 4 3 2 1

First Edition

Contents

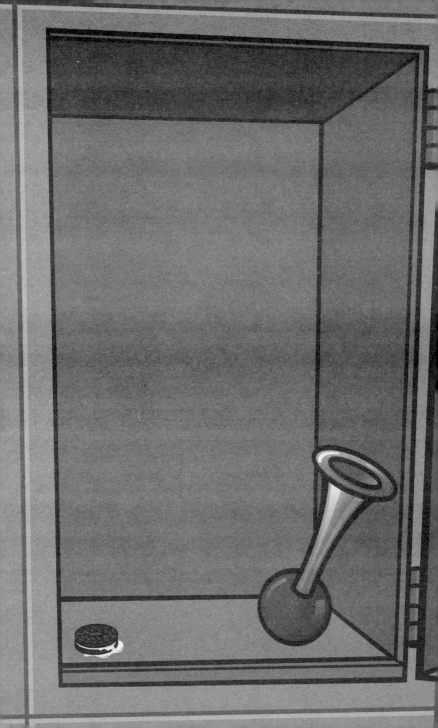

Surprise Mystery Field Trip!

My name is A.J. and I know what you're thinking. You're thinking about the future. Because that's what I'm thinking about.

I don't know what the future is gonna be like, but I know it's gonna be cool. In the future, we're going to have all kinds of awesome stuff like flying cars, jetpacks, and microwavable underwear. And we're definitely going to have virtual-reality time-machine headbands. That's for *sure*.

I can't wait until I get my virtual-reality time-machine headband. Think of it—we'll be able to travel back to any year we want! When I have my own virtual-reality time-machine headband, I know where I'm gonna go—to the year 1857. Do you want to know why? Because that was the year Joseph Gayetty invented toilet paper.

I wonder what they used before 1857.

On second thought, maybe I'll use my virtual-reality time-machine headband to travel back to *today*. Yeah! That way, I'll be able to tell myself what the future is gonna be like. It would be cool to predict the future.

I hope A.J. from the future gets here soon. Hey, maybe when he gets here, *both* of us can go back to 1857 and watch Joseph Gayetty invent toilet paper.*

My point is: it was Monday. Our teacher—Miss Banks—was late to class because there was a retirement party in the teachers' lounge for Mr. Loring. He's been the music teacher at our school for a million hundred years. I don't think music even *existed* when boring Mr. Loring started teaching. He probably taught Beethoven

---

*What are you looking down here for? The story is up *there*!

how to play the piano.

"I can't wait to see Miss Banks's new hairdo," said Alexia, this girl who rides a skateboard all the time.

"Oh, yeah," said Andrea, this annoying girl with curly brown hair. "She said she was going to the hair salon after school on Friday."

"I bet she's going to be *beautiful*," said Emily, Andrea's crybaby friend.

I couldn't care less what Miss Banks's hair looked like.

But then she walked into the classroom. Her hair was purple! Bright *purple*!

"AHHHHHHHHHHH!" we all shouted.

"Do you like it?" Miss Banks asked,

spinning around so we could get a good look at her hair.

"Yes!" said Alexia.

"Then you can have it!" Miss Banks said as she pulled a purple wig off her head and tossed it up in the air.

Miss Banks pulls lots of pranks.

"Ha-ha-ha!" she said. "Time is fun when you're having flies!"

That's Miss Banks's catchphrase. A catchphrase is something people say all the time for no reason.

"Okay everyone, it's time for math," Miss Banks told us. "Today we're going to learn about irrational numbers. An irrational number—"

She didn't have the chance to finish her sentence. You'll never believe who walked into the door at that moment.

Nobody! Why would you walk into a door? You could break your nose! But you'll never believe who walked into the door*way*.

It was Mrs. Stoker, the principal of Ella Mentry School!

"Good morning!" she said cheerfully. "Hey, do you kids know how the moon cuts its hair?"

"How?" asked Ryan, who will eat anything, even stuff that isn't food.

"Eclipse it!" she said. "Get it?"

I didn't get it. Mrs. Stoker is a joker. When she's not being our principal, she's a stand-up comedian.

"Hey," said Mrs. Stoker, "what did the limestone say to the geologist?"

"What?" asked Michael, who never ties his shoes.

"Don't take me for granite!" said Mrs. Stoker. Then she doubled over laughing and slapped her knees. Grown-ups slap

7

their knees when they think something is really funny. Nobody knows why.

We all laughed even though Mrs. Stoker's jokes weren't all that funny. You should always laugh at the principal's jokes. That's the first rule of being a kid.

Andrea started waving her hand in the air like she was trying to signal an airplane from a desert island. She got called on, *of course*.

"Mrs. Stoker," Andrea said, "do you know any jokes about psychologists? My mom is a psychologist."

Andrea is always bragging that her mom is a psychologist, whatever *that* is.

"Hmmm, let me think," said Mrs. Stoker. "Aha! Do you know why psychologists don't make any noise when they go to the bathroom?"

"Why?" asked Andrea.

"Because the *P* is silent!" said Mrs. Stoker. "Get it?"

We all laughed even though the joke wasn't all that funny.

"You've been a wonderful audience," Mrs. Stoker said as she opened the door to leave. Then she stopped. "Oh, I almost forgot why I came in here. I have big news!"

"You have a big nose?" asked Michael.

"Not nose, *news*!" said Neil, who we call the nude kid even though he wears clothes.

"I'm taking you kids on a surprise mystery field trip!" announced Mrs. Stoker.

"Oooh, where are we going?" asked Ryan.

"If I told you, it wouldn't be a surprise," said Mrs. Stoker. "Come on, follow me!"

Funderama

We all followed Mrs. Stoker outside, where the school bus was waiting.* Our bus driver is Mrs. Kormel, who is not normal.

"Bingle boo!" she said.

That means "hello." Mrs. Kormel invented

---

*Buses must be *really* patient because they spend so much time waiting.

her own secret language. Nobody knows why.

She drove us a million hundred miles. Well, it seemed like that, anyway. Finally, the bus pulled up to a building with a big sign out front that said "NBN-TV'S *Funderama.*"

"*Funderama!*" we all shouted at the same time. *Funderama* is a TV show for kids. It's on every Saturday morning. The host is this guy named Uncle Fred.

"I used to watch Uncle Fred on *Funderama* when I was little," I said.

"So did I!" said Mrs. Kormel.

Everybody watched *Funderama* when they were little. The show has been on TV for something like thirty years. I bet

George Washington watched *Funderama* when he was a kid.

"We've been invited to be part of the *Funderama* studio audience!" Mrs. Stoker said excitedly.

"So we get to watch them film the TV show?" asked Ryan.

"Live and in-person!" said Mrs. Stoker. "I met Uncle Fred at Giggles Comedy Club the other night. He gave me free tickets for you kids."

Everybody was excited. Well, everybody except me. I watched *Funderama* when I was in first grade. Now that we're in fourth grade, I'm too old for that silly stuff. *Funderama* was sure to be totally lame.

"My mother used to watch a kids' show

13

called *Howdy Doody*," Mrs. Kormel said as we got off the bus.

Everybody laughed because Mrs. Kormel said "doody." It's okay to say "duty," but we're not supposed to say "doody." Nobody knows why.

"Wait a minute," I said. "Somebody's name was *Doody*?"

"Yes!" Mrs. Kormel replied. "He lived in a town called Doodyville."

Everybody laughed again. "Howdy Doody" is probably part of the secret language she made up. Mrs. Kormel is definitely not normal.

As we walked inside the NBN-TV studio, each of us was given a name tag. The set looked like somebody's living room, with a fire in the fireplace and everything. There was a big video screen on the wall that said UNCLE FRED'S PLAYHOUSE. There must have been fifty other kids there, sitting on bleachers.

Hey, why do they call them bleachers? I guess they have to wash them with bleach after some little kids pee in their pants during *Funderama*.

We had to sit boy-girl-boy-girl, so we wouldn't talk to anybody. I had to sit between annoying Andrea and crybaby Emily.

The TV studio was filled with lights and video screens and big cameras and balloons. We waited a long time until some lady ran onto the stage.

"Good morning, everybody!" she said excitedly. "I'm Mrs. Crump, the head of the NBN-TV network. Say, kids, what time is it?"

"IT'S UNCLE FRED TIME!" we all screamed, because we've heard that a million hundred times.

"Are you kids excited?" Mrs. Crump asked.

"YEAH!" We all screamed our heads off again.

"Are we gonna have fun?"

"YEAH!"

"I-CAN'T-HEAR-YOU!"

Grown-ups are always saying they can't hear us. It's just sad. I guess that's what happens when you get old.

"YEAH!" we screamed louder.

"Are you ready?"

"YEAH!"

"Here's . . . Uncle Fred!"

Some guy held up cue cards that said WAVE and GO CRAZY, so we all waved and went crazy. The Uncle Fred theme song started playing . . .

It's Uncle Freddy time.
He loves to sing and rhyme.
He likes to dance and play.
He'll dance the day away.
He's like a little kid.
He'll make you flip your lid.
Forget about bedtime,
it's Uncle Freddy time!

Lights started flashing. Sirens went off. Everybody was screaming. It was loud!

Then Uncle Fred came bursting through a big piece of paper. He was wearing a checkered suit, funny glasses, and a silly hat.

The cue card guy held up a sign that said CLAP. We all clapped.

"Howdy, kids!" Uncle Fred shouted.

"Welcome to *Funderama*, your favorite TV show, brought to you by the good folks at Porky's Pork Sausages!"

He ran over to the door.

"This is my friend Dory!" shouted Uncle Fred. "She's a door! Say hi to Dory!"

"HI, DORY!" everybody shouted.

Uncle Fred ran over to the window.

"And this is my friend Windy," he shouted. "She's a window! Say hi to Windy!"

"HI, WINDY!" everybody shouted.

Then Uncle Fred ran over to the couch.

"And this is my friend Couchy!" he shouted. "Do you know what he is?"

Duh! He's a couch, of course. What are we, kindergartners?

"A COUCH!" everybody shouted.

"That's right!" shouted Uncle Fred. "Couchy and I watch TV together."

That's ridorkulous. Couches don't watch TV. They just sit there while you watch TV.

"Let's sing 'The Aardvark Song'!" shouted Uncle Fred.

I never heard of "The Aardvark Song," but most of the kids seemed to know the words . . .

I like to bark
in the dark
at the park
with a shark
and that's why I'm an . . .

"AARDVARK!" everybody shouted.

The cue card guy held up a sign that said GO CRAZY. We all went crazy.

"Ooooooooh," said Uncle Fred. "Who wants to open the Magic Treasure Chest today?"

"I do!" some kid shouted.

"I do!" some other kid shouted.

"I do!" a third kid shouted.

In case you were wondering, *everybody* wanted to open the Magic Treasure Chest. We were all waving our hands in the air.

Uncle Fred called on Alexia, and she came running up on the stage. There was a big treasure chest on the side. Uncle Fred gave Alexia a key ring that had a million

hundred keys on it.

"There's a secret treasure in here, Alexia," said Uncle Fred. "Maybe it's gold. Maybe it's jewels. Only one of these keys will open the padlock. If you can open it by the end of the show, you get to keep whatever is inside!"

"Oooooooh!" we all oooooohed.

Weird music started playing. Alexia tried one of the keys, but it didn't fit into the padlock. While she tried another key, Uncle Fred got up and walked to the middle of the stage. He picked up a weird-looking puppet from the couch and put it on his left hand.

"This is my good friend Joe King," said Uncle Fred. "Say hello to the kids, Joe!"

"Hi, kids!" said Joe King in a really high voice. It was obvious that Uncle Fred was doing the voice because you could see his lips moving.

"Hey, Joe," said Uncle Fred. "Would you like to see your name up in lights?"

"Sure!" said Joe King.

"Then you should change your name to EXIT!" shouted Uncle Fred. "Get it?"

The cue card guy held up a sign that said LAUGH. Everybody laughed.

"That's not funny!" said Joe King, and then Uncle Fred punched himself in the mouth with the Joe King puppet. Then Uncle Fred punched Joe King with his other hand and shouted, "Get lost, buster!"

"Get lost, buster!" is Uncle Fred's catchphrase. He says "Get lost, buster!" all the time.

Uncle Fred pretended he was mad at the Joe King puppet, and they started fighting with each other. Finally, he ripped Joe King off his hand and threw the puppet into the fireplace. Joe King burst into flames. The cue card guy held up a sign that said SCREAM.

While everybody was screaming, Andrea leaned over to Emily. "I don't approve of this violence," she said.

"Me neither," said Emily, who always disapproves of anything Andrea disapproves of.

"What do you have against violins?" I asked.

"Not violins, Arlo!" said Andrea, who calls me by my real name because she knows I don't like it. "Violence!"

I know the difference between violins and violence. I was just yanking Andrea's chain.

"Hey, kids!" shouted Uncle Fred. "Do you want to see a magic trick?"

"YEAH!"

Uncle Fred took a handkerchief out of his pocket and carefully draped it over one hand.

"Abracadabra . . . hocus-pocus," he said, staring at his arm. "Watch . . . watch . . . watch . . . WATCH . . ."

He pulled the handkerchief away and held his arm up for us to see. There was a watch on it.

"WATCH!" shouted Uncle Fred.

I didn't think it was very funny, but the cue card guy held up a sign that said LAUGH, so we all laughed. Every time Uncle Fred said anything funny, a weird horn would blow and confetti would drop from the ceiling, just in case we didn't know he told a joke.

"Hey, kids!" shouted Uncle Fred. "Do you want to sing 'Row, Row, Row Your Boat' with me?"

"YEAH!" we all screamed.

"Okay, first the girls," said Uncle Fred.

And then he started singing . . .

Row, row, row your boat,
gently down the stream.
Throw the boys overboard,
and listen to them scream.

The cue card guy didn't have to hold up any sign. We all clapped, waved, and went crazy. That's when the weirdest thing in the history of the world happened.

But I'm not going to tell you what it was.

Okay, okay, I'll tell you. But you have to read the next chapter. So nah-nah-nah boo-boo on you.

More Fun with Uncle Fred

3

I had forgotten how funny Uncle Fred was. As soon as he finished singing the boat song, he started dancing.

"It's time to do the Gerbil Dance!" he shouted.

The cue card guy held up a sign that said SHOUT. We all shouted.

"The Gerbil Dance is easy to do," said

Uncle Fred. "All you need to do is dance around like a gerbil!"

"How do gerbils dance?" some kid yelled.

"Watch me!" shouted Uncle Fred. He did this crazy dance where he hopped back and forth on each foot and stuck his fingers in his ears.

I really don't think gerbils dance like that. To tell you the truth, I don't think they dance *at all*. But it was funny. We all got up and did the Gerbil Dance while the music played. I almost fell off the bleachers.

"Uncle Fred is a knucklehead!" Ryan said when the music stopped.

Uncle Fred threw some confetti in the air and ran up into the bleachers. He stuck his microphone in some girl's face.

"Hey, Megan," he said, "what's your favorite kind of dirt?"

"Uh . . . dirty dirt?" she replied.

"Good answer!"

Uncle Fred stuck the mic in some other kid's face.

"Hey, Andrew," he said, "do you like to eat oatmeal?"

"Not really," he replied.

Uncle Fred ran over to our side of the bleachers and stuck the mic in Neil's face.

"Hey, Neil," he said. "do they call you Neil because you kneel down a lot?"

"No, that's my name," Neil replied.

"What's your last name?" asked Uncle Fred.

"Crouch."

"Neil Crouch?" said Uncle Fred. "Both of your names mean the same thing!"

The cue card guy held up a sign that said LAUGH. We all laughed.

Uncle Fred looked at my name tag and stuck the mic in my face.

"What does A.J. stand for?" he asked.

"None of your business," I told him.*

"Ooooooooh!" everybody ooooooooohed.

"Is it Alex Jabroni?" he asked.

"No."

"Is it Alphabet Jam? Is it Asteroid Jawbreaker? Angry Jacuzzi?"

"No!"

"A.J. stands for Arlo Jervis," said Andrea.

Everybody laughed. I wanted to run

---

*I didn't want all the kids to make fun of my name.

33

away to Antarctica and go live with the penguins. I hate Andrea.

"Say, who's got a good joke?" asked Uncle Fred.

A bunch of kids raised their hands.

Uncle Fred ran over and stuck the mic in some kid's face.

"Why did the man throw his clock out the window?" the kid asked.

"I give up," said Uncle Fred. "Why did the man throw his clock out the window?"

"He wanted to see time fly!" the kid said.

That is probably the oldest joke in the book. But Uncle Fred laughed like it was the funniest thing in the history of the world.

"Ha-ha-ha-ha-ha-ha!" he cackled. "Get lost, buster!"

Uncle Fred threw some confetti in the air and ran over to the side of the stage, where Alexia was trying to open the Magic Treasure Chest.

"How are you making out, Alexia?" he asked.

"Gross!" she replied. "I'm not making out! I'm trying to open the Magic Treasure Chest."

"Keep working at it!" shouted Uncle Fred. Then he sat down in a chair and picked up a book.

"Now I'm going to read you a story," Uncle Fred said. "It's called *Winnie the Pooh*."

What?!

"He's going to read a book about poo?" I whispered to Andrea.

"It's not poo!" she whispered back. "It's Pooh. There's an *H* at the end. It's a very famous book, Arlo!"

I don't care how famous it is. Why is there an *H* at the end of poo? That makes no sense at all. Poo sounds the same as Pooh. If you ask me, they should change the title of that book.

Uncle Fred read to us from *Winnie the Pooh*. It's a weird story about a teddy bear that loves honey. I wasn't really paying attention.

"The end," said Uncle Fred, and he closed the book.

The cue card guy held up a sign that said CLAP, and we all clapped. That's when I noticed that Uncle Fred was crying.

"*Winnie the Pooh* always makes me sad," he blubbered. "We'll be right back after this message . . ."

A Word from Our Sponsor

Uncle Fred is really emotional. After reading *Winnie the Pooh*, he was slobbering all over the place. He blew his nose into a tissue. Well, he blew his snot into the tissue. It would be weird to blow your nose into a tissue. Noses don't come off!

Then Uncle Fred slumped into a chair,

and some lady rushed over to give him a glass of water. Somebody else toweled off his face and fussed with his makeup.

We all looked up at the video screen.

Uncle Fred's face was up there. He was holding a box of Porky's Pork Sausages.

"Hey, kids!" he said. "Do you like pork sausages? Who doesn't, right? Well, if you like pork sausages, I have great news for you. If you send in ten box tops from Porky's Pork Sausage boxes, you could win an all-expenses-paid trip to the Porky's Pork Sausage factory in Porkville, Pennsylvania! You'll get to see how they make their amazing pork sausages.* Doesn't that sound like fun? Hey, I have an idea! Let's sing the Porky's jingle . . ."

---

*Because everybody wants to know how sausages are made, right?

If you like pork,
and sausages too,
Porky's Pork Sausage
is the sausage for you!

Well, *that* was weird.

I Asked for Watermelons!

While the commercial was playing on the screen, stagehands ran around with brooms and garbage bags cleaning up the confetti that Uncle Fred had thrown all over the place.

Mrs. Crump, the lady who was the head of the TV network, came out to talk to us again.

"Hey, kids, isn't Uncle Fred *great*?" she asked with way too much enthusiasm.

"YEAH!" we all shouted.

"I love Uncle Fred!" some kid yelled.

"Are you kids having a good time?" asked Mrs. Crump.

"YEAH!"

"I-CAN'T-HEAR-YOU!"

Sheesh. That lady really needs to get her hearing checked.

"YEAH!" we shouted louder.

"Are you ready for more Uncle Fred?"

"YEAH!"

Uncle Fred got up from his chair. He wasn't crying anymore.

"Okay, we're back," he said. "Everybody get up on your feet!"

We all stood up.

"You kids spend too much time staring at video game screens," Uncle Fred said. "Let's all do some jumping jacks!"

Ugh, I hate jumping jacks. But we had to do a million hundred of them with Uncle Fred. That guy has way too much energy for a grown-up. I almost fell off the bleachers again. I thought I was gonna die.

"Okay, on to the funny stuff," said Uncle Fred. "It's time to sing a song with Mr. Dill, the singing pickle!"

Uncle Fred played the piano while this pickle puppet sang on the video screen.

I'd be tickled
if I had a nickel
for every pickle I ever ate!
I'd ride my bicycle,
I'd pedal very quickle
past all the icicles,
and I'd never be late!

"I've been playing piano for ten years," Uncle Fred said when the song ended. "And I'm really tired! I'll tell you, it's really hard to play the piano while you're taking a shower."

A picture appeared on the screen of Uncle Fred playing a piano in the shower.

The cue card guy held up a sign that said LAUGH. We all laughed.

"Get lost, buster!" Uncle Fred shouted.

After that, Uncle Fred played an accordion. Then he interviewed a goat as if it was a person. Then we all played Simon Says. There was a tug-of-war contest too. Finally, some kids raced to see which one could blow up a balloon and then pop the balloon by sitting on it. It was exhausting just to watch Uncle Fred do his show.

"Hey, Alexia!" he shouted. "How are you making out with the Magic Treasure Chest?"

"No luck yet," she replied.

"Keep working at it!" said Uncle Fred. "Next, we're going to drop watermelons off the roof of the building and shoot a video of them as they hit the ground and explode. Doesn't that sound like fun?"*

"YEAH!"

"Follow me, kids!"

We were about to get up and follow Uncle Fred to the roof. But that's when the weirdest thing in the history of the world happened. One of the stagehands came over to Uncle Fred.

"Uh . . . Uncle Fred," he said quietly, "we couldn't get the watermelons."

"What?" replied Uncle Fred.

The stagehand looked like he was trembling with fear.

"We, uh, went shopping, and they were

---

*It is! Go on YouTube and search for "dropping watermelons."

all out of watermelons."

Uncle Fred looked really mad.

"ARE. YOU. SERIOUS?" he asked, raising his voice.

"I'm really sorry, Uncle Fred," said the stagehand. "We went to three supermarkets. They had cantaloupes, but they were

all out of watermelons. Do you want us to—"

"I ASKED FOR WATERMELONS!" Uncle Fred shouted at him. "IT DOESN'T WORK WITH CANTALOUPES! THIS IS UN-BE-LIEV-A-BLE! I WANT WATERMELONS! I NEED WATERMELONS!"

Uncle Fred's face was turning red, like the inside of a watermelon. He looked like *he* was about to explode. The stagehand backed away from him, terrified. The camera operators looked like they were scared of him too.

Then, suddenly, Uncle Fred fell on the floor and started kicking his feet, pounding the floor with his fists, and screaming like a two-year-old.

"I WANT MY MOMMY!" shouted

Uncle Fred.

I had never seen a grown-up throw a temper tantrum before. Uncle Fred was out of control! It was amazing! You should have been there! We got to see it live and in-person.

Andrea Is Annoying

A bunch of stagehands tried to calm down Uncle Fred. Mrs. Crump came over to talk to us.

"I'm terribly sorry, kids," she said. "*Funderama* is over for today. Uncle Fred isn't usually like this."

Mrs. Crump kept apologizing, and she gave us free tickets to come back and see another episode of *Funderama* whenever we want. Alexia never was able to open up the treasure chest. As we left the studio, each of us got a goody bag filled with Porky's Pork Sausages. The bus was waiting for us outside.

"So how was *Funderama*?" asked Mrs. Kormel. "Isn't Uncle Fred great?"

"He was awesome!" said Ryan.

"It was cool!" said Neil. "Uncle Fred was totally out of his mind!"

We were all talking about how much fun we had at the *Funderama* taping. The only one who didn't look happy was Little Miss Perfect. Andrea had on her frowny face.

"What's the matter?" I asked her. "Was your clog dancing lesson canceled again?"*

"Very funny, Arlo," replied Andrea. "I'm

---

* That's a kind of dance that plumbers do.

worried about Uncle Fred."

"What about him?" I asked.

"Well, my mother is a psychologist," said Little Miss Know-It-All. "And she told me that grown-ups who act like Uncle Fred have emotional problems."

"What?!" I said. "He was just upset because they didn't get him the watermelons he asked for. What's the big deal?"

"Didn't you see the way he was behaving?" asked the Human Homework Machine. "He was so immature, and hyperactive too. My mom told me it's very hard for adults like Uncle Fred to function in the real world with mature people. I think he needs to get professional help."

"Your *face* needs to get professional help," I told Andrea.

"Oh, snap!" said Ryan.

Andrea is no fun at all. Any time grown-ups act silly, she always says they need to get help. Uncle Fred is cool. He was just having a tough day.

The bus pulled up to school, and we walked a million hundred miles to Miss Banks's class. And you'll never believe who walked through the door at that moment.

Nobody! You can't walk through a door! I thought we went over that in Chapter One. But you'll never believe who walked through the door*way*.

It was us!

"I have an announcement to make," Miss Banks said as we walked into the room.

Uh-oh. When teachers make announcements, it usually means bad news. Miss Banks took a piece of paper out of her pocket.

"The Board of Education," she read off the paper, "has decided that due to poor test scores at Ella Mentry School, Halloween will be canceled this year."

What?!

"NOOOOOOOOOOO!" shouted Ryan.

"They can't do that!" shouted Alexia.

"It's not fair!" shouted Neil.

Everybody was yelling and screaming

and hooting and hollering and freaking out.

"Just kidding!" Miss Banks said as she threw the piece of paper in the garbage

can. "It's time for math. Today we're going to talk about irrational numbers."

Huh? What's that?

"An irrational number," said Miss Banks, "is a real number that can't be expressed as a fraction *blah blah blah blah blah blah* . . ."

What a snoozefest. I had no idea what she was talking about. Fourth grade is *hard*! Miss Banks went on and on about irrational numbers.

By dismissal time, I had forgotten all about our visit to *Funderama*. I had forgotten all about Uncle Fred.

But he hadn't forgotten about *us*.

There, There

When we got to class the next day, we pledged the allegiance and did Word of the Day. Then Miss Banks did the weirdest thing in the history of the world. She started spinning around in circles, skipping around the room, climbing up onto the windowsill, and doing cartwheels.

"Miss Banks," asked Andrea, "what are

you doing?"

"I'm pretending to be an irrational number," she replied. "Get it? Time is fun when you're having flies!"

Miss Banks is weird.

"As I was saying yesterday," she continued, "*blah blah blah blah blah blah . . .*"

She went on and on about irrational numbers. I thought I was going to die from old age. Finally, it was time for lunch, and then recess.

Do you know what rotini is? It's this curly pasta. We have a cool slide on our playground that looks a lot like rotini. We call it the Rotini Slide. So it has the perfect name. We were all taking turns sliding down the Rotini Slide, and you'll never believe in a million hundred years who showed up out of nowhere.

I'm not going to tell you.

Okay, okay, I'll tell you.

It was Uncle Fred!

It's true! A car pulled up to the playground; he stepped out and walked right over to us!

"Uncle Fred!" we all shouted.

"What are *you* doing here?" asked Michael.

"Can I play with you kids?" he asked.

Grown-ups *never* ask to play with us on the playground. Uncle Fred looked a little sad, and that made me feel sad too.

"Sure, you can play with us," I told him.

"Would you like to slide down the Rotini

Slide?" Alexia asked him.

"Yeah!" Uncle Fred said excitedly.

He climbed up the ladder to the top of the Rotini Slide and slid down.

"Wheeeee!" he yelled. "Look at me. I'm flying! Yippeeee!"

It was a little weird. Grown-ups aren't supposed to slide down slides, and they *never* say "Yippeeee!" That's the first rule of being a grown-up.

When he got to the bottom of the slide, Uncle Fred wanted to climb up and do it again, but Andrea grabbed him by his shoulders.

"We need to talk, Uncle Fred," she said. "How old are you?"

"I'm fifty years old," he replied.

Fifty?! Wow, that's like half a century!

"Shouldn't you be at home, Uncle Fred?" Andrea asked. "Or at the TV studio getting ready for the next episode of *Funderama*?"

"I don't *like* being at home or in the studio," Uncle Fred whined, a pout on his face. "I want to be here, playing with you kids."

"Why don't you leave him alone, Andrea?" I asked. "He's not bothering anybody."

"You're a fifty-year-old man!" Andrea told Uncle Fred. "You shouldn't be playing on a playground and acting like a little kid. Don't you think it's time for you to grow up?"*

---

*That makes no sense. You can't grow down.

"Chillax, Andrea," Neil said. "We *want* to play with him."

Uncle Fred sat at the bottom of the slide for a minute, like he was thinking over what Andrea had said. And then the weirdest thing in the history of the world happened.

He started sobbing.

"See what you did, Andrea!" I told her. "You made him feel sad."

"Yeah!" everybody agreed.

Uncle Fred was crying and slobbering all over himself. Emily took a tissue out of her pocket and gave it to him.

"No, Andrea's right," Uncle Fred said, after blowing his nose with a snort. "I shouldn't be here."

We all gathered around Uncle Fred and put our hands on his shoulders.

"I don't have any grown-up friends," Uncle Fred said sadly. "I don't fit in when I'm around grown-ups. And I'm too old to play with kids. So I don't fit in with anybody."

"You can come and play with us

anytime," said Neil.

"There, there," said Andrea, giving Uncle Fred a hug.

Why do people say "there, there" when they want to make sad people feel better? What does "there, there" mean, anyway? Where is there? And why would saying "there, there" cheer anybody up?

"All I ever wanted to do was make people happy," sobbed Uncle Fred. "I'm just a sad, pathetic clown."

And then he started in crying again.

"You're not pathetic," said Alexia, "and there's nothing wrong with being a clown."

"Yeah," added Emily. "Clowns make people happy."

Uncle Fred told us that when he was in

college he wanted to become a teacher, but he was told that he was too immature. That's why he went into children's television in the first place.

"I didn't mean to make you sad," Andrea

told him. "I just thought somebody needed to tell you the truth."

"I'm glad you did," Uncle Fred said. "From now on, I'm going to be better."

"That's great," Andrea told him. "It's okay to be silly, but sometimes, grown-ups need to act like mature adults."

Uncle Fred closed his eyes for a minute, and then he turned to us.

"But I don't know how to be a mature grown-up," he finally said. "I don't know how grown-ups are supposed to act."

That's when I got the greatest idea in the history of the world.

"I know!" I told him. "We can teach you!"

Talk Like a Grown-Up

Did you ever play the Talk Like a Grown-Up game? That's my favorite game in the world. We play it all the time. It's easy. All you have to do is talk like a grown-up.

"You can teach me how to be like a mature grown-up?" asked Uncle Fred.

"Of course we can," I told him. "It's

simple. Watch."

Ryan got up and stood in front of me.

"Hello, Ryan," I said, putting on my low man voice.

"Hello, A.J.," Ryan replied, in his own deep man voice, and we shook hands.

Grown-ups are always shaking hands with each other. Nobody knows why.

"Nice weather we've been having," I said.

"Yes," said Ryan. "They say it may rain on Friday."

"Wait a minute!" interrupted Uncle Fred. "Why are you talking about the weather?"

"Because that's mostly what grown-ups talk about," I told him. "They're *always* talking about the weather."

"Who cares about the weather?" Uncle Fred asked.

"Nobody," I explained. "Just watch and learn."

Ryan and I faced each other again.

"Do you want to play golf next week, Ryan?" I asked. Because grown-ups are always playing golf.

"That's a great idea," replied Ryan. "I need to work on my putting."

"How's business, old man?" I asked.

"I made a million dollars on Tuesday," replied Ryan.

"Well, that's inflation," I said.* "You

---

*I know all about inflation. That's when you put air in your bike tires.

should buy yourself a new car."

"Maybe I will," said Ryan. "Say, how about those Dodgers?"

"They may go all the way this season," I replied.

"The grass in my yard is getting too high," said Ryan.

"You need to mow it," I replied.

Then I turned to Uncle Fred. "See?" I said. "It's easy to talk like a grown-up!"

"But I don't care about golf or business or cars or lawns," said Uncle Fred.

"Nobody does!" I explained to him. "But grown-ups are old, so they ran out of things to say to each other a long time ago. That's why they talk about all that boring stuff. If you talk like that, you'll sound grown-up and mature."

"I just don't get it," said Uncle Fred.

"It's really simple," I told him. "Repeat after me: The rain in Maine goes mainly

down the drain."

"The rain in Maine goes mainly down the drain," said Uncle Fred.

"Good," I said. "One more time, where does the rain go?"

"Down the drain," he replied. "Down the drain."

"And where is that drain?" I asked.

"In Maine!" he replied. "In Maine!"

"I think he's got it!" Alexia shouted.

Teaching Uncle Fred how to talk like a grown-up was a great idea, if I do say so myself. No wonder I'm in the gifted and talented program.

Back to *Funderama*

When we got back to class, Miss Banks wrote the word HISTORY in big letters on the whiteboard.

"Today we're going to learn about the history of garbage cans," she told us. "The first garbage can was invented—"

But Miss Banks didn't have the chance

to finish her sentence. You'll never believe who poked her head into the door at that moment.

Nobody! Why would you poke your head into a door? Don't you ever learn? But you'll never believe who poked her head into the door*way*.

No, it wasn't Uncle Fred. Nice try, though.

It was Mrs. Stoker, the principal!

"I just wanted to see how you kids were making out," she said.

"Ugh!" we all shouted. "We're not making out!"

"We're learning about the history of garbage cans," Alexia said.

"But it's boring," said Michael.

"Well," asked Mrs. Stoker, "what do you want to learn about?"

"We don't want to learn *anything*," I said. "We want to go back to *Funderama*."

"Yeah!" said Ryan. "They gave us free tickets to come back any time we want."

"They're taping the next show this afternoon," said Alexia. "Can we go?"

"Please, please, please, please, please, please, please, please, please, please, PLEASE?" everybody shouted.

The more times you say "please," the harder it is for grown-ups to say "no." That's the first rule of being a kid.

"Well . . . okay," said Mrs. Stoker.

"I'll take you."

"YAY!" we all shouted, which is also "YAY" backward.

Mrs. Stoker called for the school bus, and we all climbed on. We were so excited, we sang the Uncle Fred theme song the whole ride over to the TV studio. Even Mrs. Stoker joined in.

"WE WANT UNCLE FRED!" we chanted when we got inside the studio. "WE WANT UNCLE FRED!"

That Mrs. Crump lady came out to talk to us.

"Hi, everybody," she said. "Welcome to *Funderama*. Hey, look under your seats."

I looked under my seat. There was a box

of Porky's Pork Sausages down there.

"You get pork sausages!" shouted Mrs. Crump, pointing at the bleachers. "And *you* get pork sausages! And *you* get pork sausages!"

The cue card guy held up a sign that said CLAP, and we all clapped.

"Say, kids, what time is it?" asked Mrs. Crump.

"IT'S UNCLE FRED TIME!" we all screamed,

"Are you kids excited?"

"YEAH!"

"Are we gonna have fun?"

"YEAH!"

"Are you ready?"

"YEAH!"

"I-CAN'T-HEAR-YOU!"

"YEAH!" we shouted louder, so she could hear us.

"Here's . . . Uncle Fred!"

The cue card guy held up a sign that said GO CRAZY. We all went crazy.

Uncle Fred came running out. He had on his Joe King hand puppet. It looked just like the one he threw into the fireplace. I guess he has a bunch of Joe King hand puppets.

"Hello, Joe," Uncle Fred said.

"Hello, Uncle Fred," said Joe King.

"Nice weather we've been having," said Uncle Fred.

"Yes," said Joe King. "They say it may rain on Friday."

"Do you want to play golf next week, Joe?"

"Yes," replied Joe King. "I need to work on my putting."

"How's business, old man?"

"I made a million dollars on Tuesday,"

replied Joe King.

"Well, that's inflation," said Uncle Fred. "You should buy a new car."

It was weird! Uncle Fred was just saying the same stuff we said when we were playing Talk Like a Grown-Up. He wasn't funny at all. Kids were looking around. I saw one kid yawn.

The cue card guy held up a sign that said CLAP. Nobody clapped.

"Borrrrr-rrrrring!" somebody yelled.

"How about some jokes?" shouted some other kid.

"Yeah, say something funny, Uncle Fred!"

"How about those Dodgers?" asked Uncle Fred.

"They may go all the way this season," replied Joe King.

"My grass is getting too high," said Uncle Fred.

"You need to mow it," replied Joe King.

The cue card guy held up a sign that said LAUGH. Nobody laughed.

"They're talking like grown-ups!" some kid shouted.

"BOOOOOOOOOOOOO!"

"Uncle Fred isn't funny anymore!" somebody shouted.

"WE DON'T WANT UNCLE FRED!" everybody started chanting. "WE DON'T WANT UNCLE FRED!"

Some kid took one of his pork sausages and threw it at Uncle Fred. He ducked to get out of the way. Then a bunch of kids started throwing pork sausages at Uncle Fred. Mrs. Crump came running out.

"STOP!" she screamed, holding up her hands.

She looked really mad! I thought she was going to yell at us for throwing pork sausages at Uncle Fred. But she didn't. Instead, she yelled at Uncle Fred.

"That's the last straw!"* Mrs. Crump shouted at him.

Huh? What did straws have to do with anything?

"Fred," she said. "You're fired!"

---

*If they run out of straws, they should just buy a new box.

"Fired? Why?" asked Uncle Fred. "What did I do?"

"You got boring!" said Mrs. Crump.

Uncle Fred looked angry, like he was going to throw another one of his temper tantrums.

"You can't fire me!" he shouted. "I'm a star! I've been doing this show for thirty years!"

Then Uncle Fred started crying again.

"I don't care how long you've been doing the show!" said Mrs. Crump. "Get lost, buster! And take that silly hand puppet with you!"

A Brilliant Idea!

We left the TV studio. Everybody was sad and angry about Uncle Fred getting fired.

"This is all your fault!" I told Andrea. "You're the one who told him he needed to act like a grown-up!"

"No, it's all *your* fault, Arlo!" Andrea replied. "*You're* the one who *taught* him how to act like a grown-up!"

"Ooooooooooh," said Ryan. "A.J. and Andrea are having a lover's spat. They must be in *love*!"

"When are you gonna get married?" asked Michael.

It was probably *all* our fault that Uncle Fred got fired. He was a famous celebrity, and we ruined his life. I felt terrible about it. I wanted to run away to Antarctica and go live with the penguins.

"Bingle boo!" Mrs. Kormel said as we got back on the bus. "Did you have fun at *Funderama*?"

"Don't ask," mumbled Andrea.

"It was a disaster," said Mrs. Stoker.

We took our seats on the bus. Nobody was talking to anybody else. We just sat there.

That's when the weirdest thing in the history of the world happened. Mrs. Kormel was about to pull out of the parking lot when we saw Uncle Fred walk out the back door of the studio. He was hanging his head and shuffling his feet as he walked slowly to his car.

"He looks so sad," said Emily. "I feel sorry for him."

Suddenly Mrs. Stoker got up from her seat.

"STOP THE BUS!" she shouted.

Mrs. Kormel slammed on the brakes. The bus screeched to a halt.

Mrs. Stoker ran off the bus and went over to Uncle Fred. We opened the bus windows, so we could hear what they were saying to each other.

"Uncle Fred!" shouted Mrs. Stoker. "We all feel terrible about what happened."

"My career is over," Uncle Fred replied sadly. "I'm finished."

"I just had a crazy idea," said Mrs. Stoker. "The music teacher at our school, Mr. Loring, just retired."

"So?" asked Uncle Fred.

"Would you have any interest in becoming . . . a music teacher?" asked Mrs. Stoker.

"What?!" asked Uncle Fred. "Me? A music teacher? Are you serious?"

"Of course I'm serious," said Mrs. Stoker. "You love music. You're great with kids. And you're extremely silly. You're just the kind of person we need to be the new music teacher at Ella Mentry School!"

Mrs. Stoker is a genius. She should get the Nobel Prize for that idea. That's a prize they give out to people who don't have bells.

"Well, uh, I . . . suppose . . . maybe, uh," said Uncle Fred, thinking it over. "Sure! I'd love to be your music teacher!"

"YAY!" we all shouted out the bus windows. That's also "YAY" backward.*

---

*Wait! Is this book going to have a happy ending? Ugh! Disgusting!

11

Pie in the Sky

When we got to school the next day, we pledged the allegiance and did Word of the Day with Miss Banks.

"Okay," she said, "take out your anatomy textbooks."

What?! I don't even know what anatomy is. We don't have any anatomy textbook.

"Just kidding," said Miss Banks. "We're going to start the day with music class!"

All of the sudden, the lights started flashing. Sirens went off. And you'll never believe in a million hundred years who ran through the door.

Nobody! You can't run through doors! Doors are made out of wood. But you'll never believe who ran through the door*way*.

It was Uncle Fred, of course! He was holding a banjo.

"It's Uncle Fred time!" yelled Miss Banks.

"Howdy, kids!" Uncle Fred shouted. And then he started playing his banjo and singing . . .

It's Uncle Freddy time.

I love to sing and rhyme.

I like to dance and play.

I'll dance the day away.

I'm like a little kid.

I'll make you flip your lid.

Forget about bedtime,

it's Uncle Freddy time!

We all sang the song again while Uncle Fred danced around like a lunatic.

"Hey, I've got an idea!" he shouted. "Let's play musical chairs!"*

Musical chairs is a weird game. The object of the game isn't to score points or

---

*That's ridorkulous. Chairs can't play music.

98

make goals like in a regular game. No, the object of the game is to sit down. Nobody knows why. But it's fun. Sometimes, you have to knock the other kids over just so you can sit in a chair.

We set up some chairs in the front of the room. While Uncle Fred started the music, Miss Banks lined up a bunch of paper plates on the windowsill. I guess we were going to have snacks after we finished playing musical chairs.

"Line up and march around the chairs," shouted Uncle Fred. "When the music stops, sit down . . . if you can!"

We all walked around and around the chairs while Uncle Fred played his banjo.

Then suddenly, he stopped.

We all dove for the chairs.

Michael was the only one who didn't get to sit down.

"Bummer in the summer!" Michael shouted.

"Sorry, Michael!" said Uncle Fred. "You're out of the game."

Uncle Fred went over to the windowsill. Miss Banks was spraying whipped cream onto the paper plates. Uncle Fred picked one of them up. And you'll never believe what happened next.

He walked over to Michael and threw the paper plate at him! It hit Michael right in the face.

"Get lost, buster!" Uncle Fred shouted.

"Oh, snap!" said Ryan.

"Why did you do that?" asked Michael, wiping the whipped cream off his face.

"That's not how you play musical chairs!"

"Oh, I forgot to tell you," said Uncle Fred. "I changed the rules."

"I can't believe you did that!" said Miss Banks. Then Miss Banks picked up a whipped cream pie and threw it at Uncle Fred.

Bam! Right in the kisser.

"I don't approve of this violence," Andrea said.

"What do you have against violins?" I asked her.

Andrea needs to get a sense of humor transplant. I picked up a whipped cream pie and threw it at her face. I got her good. She was *really* mad!

"Pie fight!" somebody shouted.

Andrea picked up a pie and threw it at me, but I ducked and it hit Emily in the face. She started crying, of course. Then Ryan threw a pie at Michael. Michael threw a pie at Alexia. Alexia threw a pie at Neil. Neil threw a pie at Andrea.*

"Help!"

"I have pie in my eye!"

"Run for your lives!"

We were all throwing pies at each other! Whipped cream was everywhere. Everybody was yelling and screaming and hooting and hollering and freaking out.

It was the best music class *ever*!

---

*Do NOT do this at your school!

Well, that's pretty much what happened. I guess grown-ups *can* be silly sometimes, and sometimes they can be mature. And sometimes, they can even act like babies. Maybe Uncle Fred will be a great music teacher. Maybe we'll find out what was inside the Magic Treasure Chest. Maybe Mrs. Crump will get her hearing checked. Maybe I'll get a virtual-reality time-machine headband. Maybe we'll learn about the history of garbage cans. Maybe A.J. from the future will come so both of us can go back to 1857 and watch Joseph Gayetty invent toilet paper.

But it won't be easy!

More weird books from Dan Gutman

My Weird School

My Weird School Graphic Novels

My Weirder School

My Weirdest School

My Weirder-est School

My Weird School Fast Facts

My Weird School Daze

My Weird Tips